TO: SOPHIA & BRIAN

Have a very Merry Christmas......
presents to all!

Oemah
CHRISTMAS 2008

Silly Sam Squirrel
and the
Brown Christmas Light Bulb

Written by Derrick LaRiviere
Illustrated by Debi Derksen

Paul Marc Enterprises Publishing.   ISBN 0-9685436-0-X.   Printed in Canada.

It was just two days before Christmas. The winter air was crisp and clear, and the night sky sparkled brightly over the town where Silly Sam Squirrel lived.

Sliding down snow banks and hopping from tree to tree, Silly Sam hurried off to meet with his best friend Tanis. The bridge overlooking the bay was their secret meeting place.

"Yoo-hoo, Silly Sam Squirrel. Come out, come out wherever you are. And please hurry, it's chilly out tonight!" called Tanis.

"Chilly you say? I should think that's not unusual with Christmas only two days away," chimed a friendly voice.

"There you are Silly Sam Squirrel! How did you sneak up on me like that?" chuckled Tanis.

"It wasn't easy," said Silly Sam.
"My glasses kept fogging up on me."

Tanis reached into her pocket for a
handkerchief and wiped off his glasses.

"That's better," said Silly Sam as he adjusted his glasses. "But I must admit, my eyesight is starting to fail me. I guess it must be old age."

"You're not getting older, you're getting cuddlier," Tanis said, as she reached up and gave Silly Sam Squirrel a big warm hug.

Forgetting all
about the cold, they
cuddled and chatted for
quite awhile that evening
before going their separate ways.

Tanis was going to their friend Jared's house.
Jared had done an extra special job of decorating
his house with Christmas lights this year, and she
couldn't wait to see them.

Silly Sam was on his way to the other
side of town. One of his oldest and
closest squirrel friends had
invited him over for
a Christmas visit.

"Oh,
I almost forgot,"
Tanis said, as she reached
into one of her pockets. "Here, I brought
you some of your favorite nuts."

"Oh, thank you," said Silly Sam
as he put the nuts Tanis gave him into his nut pouch.
"Mmmmm, yummy, yummy," he said, smacking his lips.

He waved goodbye to Tanis as he watched her stroll
down the path that led to Jared's house.

Jared was so excited about
showing Tanis his Christmas lights,
that he was waiting outside to greet her.

"Ta-da!" sang Jared, as he gestured proudly
towards his brightly lit house.

"Oh wow," exclaimed Tanis. "You must have hung
a ka-zillion lights on your house Jared!"

Then Tanis stopped in her tracks. She stopped talking, stopped walking and started gawking. Her eyes were as big as two silver dollars.

"Oh look! That one is my favorite!" said Tanis as she pointed to the Brown Christmas Light Bulb on the top of Jared's house.

"I was hoping you would notice it," chuckled Jared. "It's the only one in the whole world and I made it especially for Santa Claus."

"You made it for Santa?"
questioned Tanis. "How come?"

"Well, I was afraid that Santa
wouldn't know which house I
lived in," said Jared. "So I wrote him a
letter and told him to drop off all my presents at
the house with the Brown Christmas Light Bulb on it.
That way he wouldn't miss my house on Christmas Eve."

Tanis agreed it was a great plan which was sure to
work. But little did they know things were about to change.

Later that evening, Silly Sam Squirrel passed by Jared's house on his way home from Christmas visiting. That's when he saw the Brown Christmas Light Bulb for the first time. Because of his poor eyesight, he had mistaken it for a big juicy nut.

He hopped up to the top of Jared's house and grabbed it with his little paws.

"Mmmm, yummy, yummy. I'll eat you for Christmas dinner!" said Silly Sam Squirrel, smacking his lips louder than ever. He put the Brown Christmas Light Bulb in his nut pouch and made his way home.

The next night was Christmas Eve. When Tanis learned
that Jared's Brown Christmas Light Bulb was missing, she
phoned Silly Sam Squirrel to help them look for it.

"Silly Sam, we really need your help!" blurted Tanis. "We
have to find it tonight before Santa comes!"

"You can count on me,"
said Silly Sam. "I'll be right over."

The three of them began looking high and low for the Brown Christmas Light Bulb.

Jared thought it might have rolled under the big spruce tree, but the bunnies had already checked under there.

Tanis hoped the cardinals would have spotted it from high in the trees. Sadly, they reported seeing no sign of it anywhere.

Silly Sam poked his head through the hollow log nearby.
"We haven't seen any Brown Christmas Light Bulbs lately,"
chattered the chipmunks.

"Where could it be?" they all wondered.
They were running out of luck and running out of time.

"If we don't find it soon, I won't get any presents from Santa Claus," complained Jared. He started feeling very sad, and his lower lip started to tremble at the thought of not having any presents to open on Christmas morning.

"Where is my Brown Christmas Light Bulb?" moaned Jared as he started to cry. It was so cold his tears froze into little ice cubes, which made a sad tinkling sound when they hit the ground.

"Don't cry," said Tanis. "Christmas is the best time of year even without presents."
"It is?" sniffled Jared.

"That's right," said Silly Sam Squirrel. "Christmas is that special time of year when family and friends get together to count their many blessings, and to celebrate baby Jesus' Birthday. He was born to bring peace and goodwill to everyone in the world. That's what Christmas is really all about."

"Oh yeah," said Jared thoughtfully. "I guess somehow I had forgotten about that."

Jared looked
up at the stars in the
heavens above him, slowly
stopped crying and began to think.

As he thought more and more about baby Jesus, his
family, his friends and the true meaning of Christmas, a smile
tugged at the corners of his mouth. And that smile began to
grow. It grew bigger and Bigger and BIGGER!

"I know what I'll do! I'll make this my best Christmas ever," he said. "Even without presents."

"Wow! That's the spirit!" said Tanis. "I'm very proud of you Jared."

"I think we should celebrate!" said Silly Sam, reaching into his nut pouch.

"Here Jared, I was saving this big juicy nut for Christmas dinner, but I want you to have it." He handed it to Jared.

Jared was beaming. He couldn't believe his own eyes.

"Oh Silly Sam Squirrel, you really are silly. That's not a big juicy nut. That's my Brown Christmas Light Bulb!"

"Hooray!" they all shouted. "Three cheers for Sam! Three Cheers for Sam!" They were all so happy, they were bouncing with excitement.

All three
of them held
hands and danced
in a circle in the
moonlit snow,
laughing and singing,
laughing and singing…

It really was the
best Christmas ever,
presents and all.